WOODY AND JUNE VERSUS THE CHASE

WOODY AND JUNE VERSUS THE CHASE

WOODY AND JUNE VERSUS THE APOCALYPSE, EPISODE 8

ROBERT J. MCCARTER

LITTLE HUMMINGBIRD PUBLISHING

Woody and June versus the Chase

Woody and June versus the Apocalypse, Episode 8

Cover photography © tristanbnz, depositphoto.com

"Zombies Ahead" image by ducu59us

Version 1.0, September 2022

ISBN: 978-1-941153-64-2

Find out more about this book at: WoodyAndJune.com

Visit Robert's website at: www.RobertJMcCarter.com

Published by:

Little Hummingbird Publishing

P.O. Box 23518

Flagstaff, AZ 86002

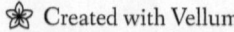 Created with Vellum

CHAPTER ONE

THE TRUTH IS, I'm scared. Terrified.

Not of Talia, not of that mess we just left at Phantom Ranch down at the bottom of the Grand Canyon, but of the future.

June and Dallas are in the back of the beautiful new-when-the-apocalypse-happened Toyota crew cab 4x4 chatting away like they're a couple of girlfriends excited about brunch... or something like that. Knowing June, it would be a gun and for Dallas it would be something like bungee jumping, but you get the idea.

The smell of our sweaty, dirty bodies doesn't quite overcome the new-car smell, and if you look at the desert whipping by out the window with its cacti and shrubs you might, for a moment, convince yourself that everything is normal. That the zombies hadn't come and that civilization hadn't crumbled. That I just landed the woman of my dreams in June and have a new best friend in Dallas and everything is okay.

But it is not.

Odds are Talia is going to come after us and the smartest way out of here fast is back through Flagstaff, but after outsmarting the local psychotic, petty, wannabe warlord there, twice, that would not be safe at all.

So, we have to embark into the unknown.

A couple of weeks ago it was just me, just getting by, nothing to lose but my own life. Now it's—

"What's going through that crazy head of yours?" June asks. I glance in the rearview mirror and see her delicate nose and her ocean-blue eyes, a quirky smile on her round face. She's leaning towards the center of the truck and I can see her clearly.

The girls had stopped talking and I hadn't even realized it.

"Yeah?" Dallas asks and I can see the mischievous smile on her face deepening her already deep smile lines. "Are you thinking about last night when you and June finally got to be alone... in a room... with a bed...?"

June punches Dallas in the arm and my cheeks flush hot and I want to say anything but what I was thinking but... June. She wants the truth out of me. Actually, after the shit that went down getting away from Talia and how before that June faked her death via zombie just to get away from Talia, I think she needs the truth from me.

I focus on the road because I don't want to see their faces and say, "I was just thinking about how glad I am to have you two in my life and how that terrifies me because now I have something worth losing."

Dead silence.

We're out of the national park on Route 64 heading roughly southeast. The pinon trees have disappeared and the brush has taken over. The Little Colorado River canyon is just visible to the north, a wide crack jagging through the landscape. It's rough, dry land and starkly beautiful.

If we're not going to Flagstaff, this is the only way we can go.

Dallas sniffs and says, "Well that does it, June. You get tired of him and he's mine. You hear? All mine."

"Not much danger of that," June says quietly. "He's mine." My cheeks burn even more.

"Yeah," Dallas says, a laugh in her voice, "because we've already established that baseball-boy here can't handle the both of us." She slaps my shoulder and sits back laughing.

More blushing on my part. I rub at my apocalypse beard to hide my face a bit, but I don't say anything. And, yeah, as long as Dallas is around, I will be teased mercilessly. At this point, after so long surviving alone, I am just fine with it.

The desert whips by and it's silent in the truck, in what amounts to our home, with just the wind and the buzz of the tires on the dirty blacktop.

"So, how are we getting to the White Mountains?" June askes after the silence is just about driving me crazy.

And it's a good question. We can't go through Flagstaff and I have stated a strong desire to stay off the Navajo reservation as much as possible.

This might just be a fantasy, but I figure the Navajo know what they are doing. They know how to grow corn in the desert, they know how to survive on a lot less than the rest of us. They have a culture and traditions that include their people surviving on this land for thousands of years.

Also, part of my fantasy is them not taking kindly at all to a white man like me just blithely wandering through after hundreds of years of men who look like me treating them so poorly.

"Carefully," I say.

"Plan, please," June counters.

June always wants to know the plan. We had a bit of an adventure (i.e., we almost died) bushwhacking into the Grand Canyon while pursued by hundreds of Zs. My plan. One we stumbled through without me sharing it and now all my plans must be articulated.

"My plan is that right now we go back to Wupatki National Monument and stay where we were before you wanted me to prove my fungus theory of zombies by dissecting one."

We had gone to Desert View Overlook at the Grand Canyon and taken out a Z and I had showed her the cauliflower-looking thing in the Z's head and the weird white fungal veins running through its body.

"That is so gross," Dallas says.

And it is. And if I was a scientist and wasn't so busy trying to survive, this is something I'd like to know more about. If we understood how the Zs worked, they would be easier to defeat.

"And then..." June prompts.

"After dark we launch a drone," I say. "Find out if there are any living near and decide on our route from there."

She's quiet for a moment as she turns it over in her head. "Alright. Good plan."

"Is dinner part of this plan?" Dallas asks with a loud yawn. "Because I need dinner."

Eating-wise, Dallas had it good down at Phantom Ranch with Talia and her "Phantom Company." They had plenty of water, they were growing food. I would never say that Dallas is overweight, but she's not as thin as June and me. She's not as used to scrounging and getting by on very little food.

"Oh, yeah," I say. "You can go catch us a rabbit and I'll cook it up for you, real nice."

I adjust my red Diamondback baseball cap. It's a little uncomfortable still, the new part Talia gave me when she tried to blow my head off is a scabby mess. It was only June's intervention that kept my head on my shoulders.

And that's the way of this time. We've all saved each other's lives. Multiple times. And I have no doubt we'll be doing it again. And soon. It's the definition of friendship in the apocalypse, saving each other. Body and soul.

"In your dreams, Woody," she says with a laugh. "Now be quiet and drive, I'm going to take a nap."

I was still terrified, but I wasn't alone. I drove while the two people most important to me in this post-apocalyptic world slept.

CHAPTER TWO

THE DRONE IS BUZZING high above us in the dark desert night, the Milky Way a glittering trail of diamonds. It's the last half of May and the spring evening has snapped cold even in the desert.

We are camped out at the end of a long dusty road in Wupatki National Monument, rough desert hills rising above us, the Little Colorado River a hundred yards away, where it is flanked by deciduous trees sucking at the scant muddy water running through.

The river is why we are here. It's why the Anasazi settled here thousands of years ago and left the ruins that are central to this monument. Water is life.

We've got jackets on against the chill. I've still got my green army supply jacket with my seed packets tucked into the inside pocket.

Seeds equal a sustainable future. It's a symbol for me like the red Diamondbacks baseball cap that's almost always on my head. That hat is a symbol of the past, of the best of the world that used to be. To me at least.

Sure, the seed packets are pretty worn and the hat has a nice hole in it from where Talia tried to blow my head off, but the symbols endure and are important.

Dallas is pacing restlessly on the dirt road, kicking at the stones in the thin lantern light. It didn't end up being much of a dinner, we are having to ration what food we have, but there is more on her mind than the fullness of her stomach.

June is sitting in the truck bed with me on top of all of our gear. She's got her hands wrapped around my arm and is leaning against me peering at the dark and grainy display of the tablet that shows us a live feed of the drone's camera.

We're looking for signs of life. Or at least that's what I'm supposed to be doing. I'm lost in her scent, sweaty and somehow still sweet, feeling the warmth of her body, wishing we had time and space to fully express our growing affection for each other.

And, yeah, these are dire times. But if I can't take a moment to appreciate the beautiful woman that loves me, then what the hell does any of this matter?

"Well?" Dallas asks from the road.

"You in a rush, Lonestar?" I ask. "Lonestar" is my nickname for her. Born in Texas, raised in Montana, wild as hell. It fits her.

"Yes, Diamondback," she says with a huff. "I'm in a hurry. Talia is coming and we are just sitting here while you guys do some heavy petting up there."

Dallas has a lot of nicknames for me. The Flagstaff psychotic, petty, wannabe warlord dubbed me "Diamondback" and she likes that one. And recently it's been the "boy" suffix. Baseball-boy, Dynamite-boy, Lovesick-boy.

"She's right," June adds. "Talia won't be able to reestablish her leadership of Phantom Company with us out here."

"With us *alive*, you mean," Dallas says, kicking at the road.

"I get that," I say, staring at the grainy display, the camera not doing well in the darkness. The screen clearly shows altitude and direction, but the camera's display is just black with flashes of grey flowing through. "But Talia is not the only danger here. The White Mountains are a long ways away, and if we stay away from the living we'll be much better off."

"There," June says with a sudden intake of breath.

The screen is still dark when I look. "Where?"

She shrugs, her body moving against mine. "Two seconds ago. Take the drone back to wherever it was."

Not that I know. With nothing on the display it's hard to orient, but I do a slow sweep, watching the compass on the display and... there it is. A light to the southeast. It's either very dim or a very long ways away.

I swivel the drone around, making sure I have the bearing right, and take it up a few hundred feet more.

Same light. Same place. Still small.

I pull out a map. "I think that's Leupp, maybe twenty miles as the crow flies. For us to see it, that's got to be quite a bit of light."

"What's in Leupp?" June asks.

I shrug. "It's on the Navajo reservation. Desert. Houses. A gas station. Not much."

"So we stay away from Leupp," Dallas says. "Can we go now?"

They're both staring at me. In some ways it makes sense to drive at night. We can drive a few miles. Launch the drone. Check for lights. As long as the batteries hold out.

That assumes that the living will have lights on and then that leaves us dealing with the stray Zs that might be out here in the dark.

All of that weighed against the imminent threat of Talia.

"How's she going to find us?" I ask.

They just stare at me.

It's a big state and it has never been hard to get lost in Arizona.

"She will," Dallas says, her arms crossed.

"Without a doubt," June adds.

It's a bit of a stretch for my logical brain, but my gut? Yeah, it agrees with them. Talia *will* find us. Someday. And we need to be ready.

"Let's compromise," I say, triggering the drone to come back. "I've got another battery for the drone charged. Let's drive a few miles, check, drive some more. When the drone is out of juice, we sleep."

Dallas kicks at the road again and mumbles her assent. June kisses me on the cheek, my reward for a clearly articulated plan.

CHAPTER THREE

DURING THE NIGHT, with our drone checks, we drive back to the paved road and head towards Sunset Crater Volcano National Monument.

The two monuments abut each other, the latter at a slightly higher elevation with ponderosa pine trees and long lava flows that are jet black and look like crumbled up brownies. Sunset Crater and smaller cinder cones rise up out of the land marking the relatively recent (geologically speaking) volcanic activity that characterizes this part of Northern Arizona.

Cinder cones and plentiful cinders stretch east and south from the San Francisco Peaks for miles.

On the south side of Sunset Crater is an unmarked dirt road that heads into an area of private land known around here as "the 40s."

The name comes from the rough lot size out here. Forty-acre parcels give or take. No paved roads. No utilities. Off-the-grid living in the high desert.

The private land is checkerboarded with state land in square-mile chunks. So there is a lot of open land interspersed with the scattered houses.

The dirt roads out here are not on any maps and they don't make any sense. They wind over the volcanic and sandy soil through the high desert past the kind of place "survivalists" loved. Because of that public/private checkerboard and the road sticking to the private squares, the roads go through some strange and hard to understand gyrations.

I had forgotten about this area. My old man dragged me out here on one of our visits. Some guy he knew that worked at the university had built himself a straw bale house.

And now that I am remembering it, it seems like a nearly perfect place to lie low for a while.

The reason we are here is because it is a way to get around the east side of Flagstaff and back to I-40 so we can hightail it towards the White Mountains. It's the only way.

The road that loops through the two monuments briefly goes through private land and the turnoff into the 40s is unmarked and unremarkable unless you know it is here. We miss it several times in the dark. Once we find it, we drive down a bit, stop, and sleep for a few hours and start up again before the sun is up, the light thin and grey, making the shrubby junipers look sinister.

"I don't like this," Dallas says quietly from the backseat. June is up front with me today staring at the map we have, which doesn't have any of these roads on it, and working the GPS on an old phone.

The land out here is generally sloping downward with distant views of the Painted Desert to the south and cinder cones to the north. The gently rolling land is filled with small juniper trees and a smattering of cacti.

The roads have been twisting around, making us backtrack a lot, but that is not what makes it strange. We keep expecting to run into something. Zs. The living. Something. But we've only seen ravens, a couple of rabbits skittering off over the dry land, and a coyote in the distance.

We've seen some buildings, a few trailers hidden behind trees that had clearly seen better days even before the apocalypse, but nothing up close.

And then we see a straw bale house.

They are called that because inside the adobe-finished walls are full bales of straw making the walls thick and providing excellent insulation.

This house is a plain rectangle with a low roof, the door hanging open and the windows broken. There's a rough shed and an outhouse next to it. Solar panels hunker on the roof and a large steel water tank sits a few yards away. A scraggly juniper crouches next to it, its branches particularly twisted and looking like it has gnarled hands reaching for the house.

I stop the truck and stare. Something isn't right.

"What's wrong?" June asks, looking at me.

I shrug. I can't explain it. Since it all went to shit, you see plenty of houses with open doors and broken windows. Most of the world is abandoned now and falling into disrepair.

I shut the truck off, secure my Diamondbacks baseball cap on my still-sore head, and get out.

"Where the hell are you going, Diamondback?" Dallas asks.

"Something isn't right," I say quietly, pulling my baseball bat from the back of the truck and checking the gun holstered on my side.

Dallas grumbles, folds her arms, and stares while June gets out the other side and draws a pistol.

We don't talk. Not wise to talk. You can draw the attention of the living and the dead.

We go slowly around the house, giving it a wide berth. Sightlines are good here, there aren't but a few of those scraggly junipers and we can see thirty yards in any direction before the rolling of the land cuts our view off.

The soil is sandy and loose, the kind that holds footprints for a while. And there is a lot of evidence of foot traffic, as you would expect, but nothing fresh, debris having been blown over the tracks we see.

No bodies. No zombies. No trash either. This place was well cared for.

After we circle all the way around, we peer in the open door. It's dark inside and we can't see much, but I don't smell much either, just a whiff of damp, musty air floating out.

I pull a flashlight from my belt and click it on, stepping closer. June is to my right and just behind me. I can hear her breathing, smell her scent.

I smile, for just a moment. We didn't have to have a long conversation. I didn't have to explain myself, she's just here by my side. My partner. I smile because this moment, more than most, demonstrates that I'm not alone anymore.

I put the small flashlight in my mouth, get a good grip on the baseball bat, and step into the doorway, June and her gun right next to me.

I take a deep breath through my nose of the cooler air. Beyond that vaguely musty smell, I don't smell anything.

We give it a moment, letting our eyes adjust. This is a one-room house. A bed against one wall, a small kitchen against another. A couch and a few chairs. A couple of closets.

And it's been ransacked. Quickly and chaotically. Crap is thrown everywhere. Someone went through here as fast as they could and pulled out everything of value.

We do a brief search and find nothing worth taking. The bedding and couch show signs of rodents living in it. It's been months since the place was cleaned out.

Again, this is not that unusual. Survivors are always scrounging. But still it doesn't feel right.

"What's on your mind, Woody?" June asks.

I grit my teeth and shake my head. "We're not in a regular neighborhood. We're in the middle of nowhere. Who would come out here and do this?"

June shrugs. "Let's go check out another house."

And we do. We wind our way through the rough, often barely-there roads, and find the same story over and over. Houses that are perfectly suited for waiting out the apocalypse that have been efficiently stripped of everything of value, all around the same time judging by the aged tracks.

Two hours later, the three of us are standing in front of a bigger straw bale house, this one built in the shape of an L, and it is a bit different. Old tracks, but bullet holes in the wall, and a corpse out front. It's just a skeleton now, sinew and ragged bits of clothing clinging to the white bone, old enough to not smell too bad. The skeleton has a gun gripped in his hand and a bullet hole in his head.

"Shit," I say quietly.

"Shit" is the universal word of the apocalypse. There are rarely any occasions where it doesn't apply, where it doesn't help convey the mood of the moment.

Dallas stays out front while June and I walk the perimeter. This house has a metal roof and a water tank for storing rainwater, a separate garage, and a greenhouse with broken windows that has a bunch of dead tomato plants in it.

This right here is where you wanted to be when the shit went down. But someone came and someone took it all away from the skeleton still holding his gun.

The sun has just peaked above the horizon and a breeze has kicked up, bringing the dusty smell of the desert.

We circle all the way around to Dallas and I swear again.

"Let's go in," June says.

I nod, stuff my flashlight in my mouth, and we walk in. It was ransacked just like the other straw bale houses, but there are three more corpses in here. A woman and two kids. All of them shot in the head. The woman still clutching a rifle.

Dallas curses with great fluency and excuses herself saying, "I'll be the lookout."

This is a nice house with a combined kitchen and living area, two bedrooms, even a bathroom with a bulky composting toilet.

June and I poke around, but all foodstuffs are gone. All useful tools have been taken, except for one thing.

"They left the guns," June says. We're still in the house near the front door having completed our search, the skeletons of the mother and children right in front of us.

I nod. It's odd because they took everything else that was usable. "Maybe it's a warning to people like us, telling us to move on, telling us that they'll be back, telling us our guns won't be enough."

She sighs and says, "I guess."

"We'll never know," I say.

She turns and nods at me, "This is so messed up it can only be the work of..." she begins.

"A psychotic, petty, wannabe warlord," I finish.

"And we know him, don't we?" she asks, her blue eyes fierce.

I nod. It only makes sense. It has to be the guy that captured us at the top of Mount Elden right after June and I met. Dallas and I also ran into him when we were leaving Flagstaff to rescue June from Talia at the Grand Canyon.

His name is Brown. Short. Stocky. And loving the apocalypse.

"Asshole," June spits. That is actually her name for him. While I thought of him as Mr. Short and Stocky before I knew his actual name, June has always thought of him as Asshole. It wasn't until our last encounter that we found out his real name.

He's got control of the east side of Flagstaff and is obviously a local. He came out here and cleaned the place out knowing that these folks would have a lot of useful gear. He and his men—I saw no women that were part of his group—killed everything, the living and Zs alike.

June has the right name for him.

And we've got to get the hell out of the area without running into him again.

CHAPTER FOUR

I HAVE rules for the apocalypse, things I try to accomplish each and every day. One is totally obvious and the second one is totally necessary and the third one is a new addition.

Rule 1: Survive. Because, yeah, you don't get another day if you don't survive. Survival, it's what the apocalypse is all about. Someone should make a T-shirt with that on it.

Rule 2: Laugh. What is life without some kind of joy, some kind of fun?

Rule 3: Spend time with June. Because when life gifts you with love, you simply must be there for it.

Our day slowly making it through the 40s is full of Rule 1 and Rule 3 and completely devoid of Rule 2. It's just too creepy.

We check out a few other homes. Send up the drone a few times to look for signs of life and help us navigate. But it's all the same. We find more ransacked homes, not a one of them left whole, more corpses, some with holes in their heads that appeared to have been living when they died, and skeletons with more damage that must have been Zs.

The day is building up on us, weighing us down. We are talking less, constantly looking around. Worried that we are not seeing any

Zs because it's not normal. And if it's not normal we don't know what to expect.

We have found a different kind of house, one that would be heaven right about now if someone hadn't trashed it. It sits up on a cinder hill, large, south-facing windows along the entire front and a big indoor planter along those windows that is overgrown and weedy but has all kinds of plants growing in it. Peppers. Tomatoes. Watermelon.

There is a sloped roof for catching rain and a water tank inside that gurgles as it circulates water, the solar power still working. It's finished in reddish-brown adobe and has earth bermed against it on three sides. Except for the front windows it blends in fairly well with the land.

I remember my father talking about these kinds of houses. They are called Earthships, the thick walls are old tires filled with dirt and result in the walls being gently curved with no sharp right angles. They called it a "ship" for a reason. It was meant to be as self-sustaining as possible. The house holds its temperature, gathers your water, and helps grow your food.

As the sun sinks behind the cinder cone, we park the truck out of the way behind the house so it is not visible.

Some of the windows are broken and the door was left open so it's clear some animals have been living in here, but it's... well, it's just about perfect.

"We can't drink the water, can we?" Dallas asks after we've explored the place and are back in the living room where June is rooting in the planter.

I shake my head. "It's been circulating, so it's probably fine, but it's not a chance I'm willing to take."

When we first escaped Talia and hiked to the North Rim of the Grand Canyon, we found some Zs that were brand new and weren't injured. They had been drinking out of a water tank that had some white fungus growing in it, the same white strands you find in a freshly killed Z.

"But we can eat these tomatoes," June says with a girlish squeal, putting a cherry tomato in my hand and then dancing over to Dallas and giving her one. She is prancing, looking like a faerie with her pixie haircut and her light dancer steps—that is if you ignore the gun on her belt and the rifle slung on her back.

That food is still growing in here in May at this elevation is a testament to how amazing these Earthships are. I smile and bite into the tomato. It isn't quite ripe, but the flesh is firm and it is sweet and is the best thing I've eaten in a long time.

Any fresh food in an apocalypse.

As June keeps darting into the overgrown planter and coming up with edible food, I stare out the windows. Just visible is a paved road, a few abandoned cars on it, debris building up. I pull out my map, consult the GPS on our old phone, and breathe a sigh of relief.

That is Leupp Road. We made it through the 40s. And I can see no activity.

"Any objections to spending the night here?" I ask, turning to find that the girls have found a decent blanket and are laying us out a picnic on the floor in front of the planter. Fresh vegetables from the garden along with a can of beans and a power bar. This is what you would call a post-apocalyptic feast.

Dallas looks at me like I'm crazy and June's head is back in among the overgrown plants and I just have to laugh.

I feel the ever-present tension in my shoulders ease, and I take a deep breath. It feels like the first I've taken in a long time.

If it wasn't for Mr. Brown, aka Mr. Short and Stocky, aka Asshole, being such a psychotic, petty, wannabe warlord, this might be it. A stopping point. A place to make a stand and try to build a life.

"Maybe we should spend a few days here," I say.

And then June isn't in the plants anymore but is on her tiptoes kissing me. Hard. That is most definitely a yes, the best kind of yes.

"Come on, guys," Dallas says from the picnic blanket. "Have some respect for the old spinster here and let's at least eat. I'll take first watch up on the roof and then you two can make like rabbits down here."

Our lips part and we are both laughing. Because we are not alone. Because we have Dallas and food and a roof for the night.

We do stay a few days, and it is the biggest mistake we could have made.

CHAPTER FIVE

LEUPP IS due east of us now and just a little closer than when we were in Wupatki National Monument. The night is dark and the drone shows the light there on the grainy display.

It's past 2:00 a.m. and I'm up on the gently sloped roof of the Earthship. The moon has gone down and the Milky Way is bright above me. It's cold, just a few degrees above freezing, and so very still. June is downstairs sleeping and Dallas is sacked out on the roof a few feet away, burrowed in her sleeping bag, gently snoring.

I'm happy. In some ways I'm as happy as I've ever been. Yes, there is much to grieve and the future is tenuous, but one of the lessons of the apocalypse is to appreciate what you have when you have it.

Any joy in an apocalypse (provided you're not hurting someone else for it).

And my joy is June.

The thought lights up my mind, the memory of her flesh against mine fresh and bright, her scent still filling my nose. It's almost like I'm a teenager falling in love for the first time. Except I know how precious it is.

To the west, twenty or so miles away is Flagstaff. I send up the drone as high as I dare and do see some lights there, but it is diffuse and not really useful.

In between Flagstaff and Leupp? Nothing. No lights. It seems like Brown and company have cleaned the area out. And that makes my stomach tight and brings the tension back into my shoulders.

I mean, it's good for us, right at this moment, being here with no living and no undead. But the cruelty of it makes me want to be cruel to him.

And I don't want to trade cruelties with another human being. Which is why I want to get us to the White Mountains.

From here, the best way to do that would be to continue east to Leupp and then head down to I-40. But the living are there, and despite all my fantasies about the Navajo and Hopi doing well in the apocalypse, it's just not wise.

I hear movement and a sweet feminine yawn as June climbs up on the roof dragging her sleeping bag.

"What are you doing up here?" I whisper.

In the darkness I can just see her shrug. "I missed you."

Tears spring to my eyes and I'm glad it's dark. "I missed you too."

"For the love of all that is sacred and holy," Dallas growls from her sleeping bag. "Was four hours alone in a room not enough for you two?"

"No," I say.

"Not even close," June says with an unusually girlish giggle.

Dallas grumbles again and turns away from us. June kisses me sweetly and lays her sleeping bag down next to me. I sit there and watch over the two things most precious to me in this insane world and let myself feel the joy.

WE DON'T TALK about leaving.

The fresh vegetables hit our undernourished systems a little hard, so we pull out the propane stove and Dallas makes us a stew with the vegetables, dried meat, and even a few potatoes June finds in the garden.

We eat and have picnics inside during the day. We all sleep and rest and recover from all we've been through, my poor blistered feet finally getting a chance to heal up. The wound to my head that Talia delivered when she tried to put a bullet in my brain starts to itch. We spend the nights up on the roof and each night the drone tells me the same thing.

This isn't the White Mountains, but it is the life I was hoping for. But it can't last. We need more food. We need water we can trust. We need to be free enough to move around and hunt. But it is precious peace and we all know it.

And we know we should be moving on but we're too tired. We're so relieved to have some comfort and some time. We are so stupid.

On our third morning there, the cold air driving me deep into my sleeping bag, I feel an arm around me and warm breath against my ear.

June. My June.

In the brief, tenuous moments as consciousness returns, I am so happy and all I wish for is more of this simple life.

She whispers in my ear, but it's not sweet nothings. "Don't sit up and don't make any noise," she whispers.

I'm awake then. I'm much better at waking up than I used to be. The apocalypse is my coffee, all the stimulation I need most days. I nod and open my eyes, the sky above the deepest blue of the coming dawn with only a few stars still visible.

"You need to see this," she whispers, her lips cold against my ear but her breath warm. "Turn over and crawl to the edge of the roof."

We haven't been sleeping in the house. In this new world it feels too exposed. Up on a roof feels safe since the Zs can't climb.

I crawl across the roof following June to the edge. Dallas is already there with binoculars pressed to her face. Everyone with coats and hats on, our breaths forming brief clouds in the cold morning as we exhale.

We're up a little ways on a cinder cone so we have a good view of the land. The soil is dark, stained nearly to the color of coal from all the cinders, with streaks that edge towards red here and there. The land is covered in short, dried grass, the light yellow contrasting with the dark soil. There are only a few scrubby junipers and the land has a moonlike feel to it.

Down on Leupp Road, a big pickup pulling a horse trailer has just stopped. There's something that's just not right about the trailer. It's rocking slightly as if something or somethings are moving in it.

"Shit," I mumble, once again greeting the day with the official word of the apocalypse.

Down the road, I see headlights and another truck with a large horse trailer coming. It goes around the first one and then turns down a dirt road. Not the road that leads to this house, but close.

It stops, a beefy man gets out, waves to the first truck, and then cranks up the trailer and unhooks it.

"We need to leave," Dallas whispers. "Now. Whatever this is, it ain't good."

"We can't," June whispers back. "They'd see us."

Our Earthship home with its fine view has a driveway that is visible from the road.

Both trucks unhitch the horse trailers and pull back onto the road and just sit there. Waiting.

The trailers, both of them, are rocking a little. There can only be one thing in there. "Zs," I whisper.

"Confirmed," Dallas hisses. "I just saw one of them stick their hand out."

The road is a couple hundred yards away and Dallas has a better view of the situation with the binocs. My stomach is tight and I want to do nothing but run. No one knows we're here, but at the same time I am sure that this is about us. But how can it be?

A few minutes later, a black Jeep heads down the road, drives past the two pickups, turns around, and pulls behind them.

A tall woman steps out, a blond ponytail sticking out from under a camo-colored beanie. She's dressed in jeans and a leather jacket, a gun on her hip, and strides quickly towards the horse trailer.

Beside me June tenses and then Dallas swears softly.

Talia.

Someone else gets out of the Jeep. A man, short and pudgy with glasses. He pulls some gear out of the Jeep, a long pole and a hard-backed suitcase, and follows Talia to the horse trailer.

If I wanted to run before, I really want to run now.

No one speaks. We don't dare. I look at June and her blue eyes are wide, her mouth hanging open just a bit. Her rifle is beside her, but she doesn't go for it and I don't say anything.

Back when we had just escaped Phantom Ranch and it became clear that Dallas had been sent after us. After June had pistol-whipped Dallas and I was so afraid she was going to kill her, she looked at me with those ocean-blue eyes of hers and said, "We're not like them."

Which is why June doesn't grab her rifle. Well, that and a two-hundred-yard shot is pretty tough. And June served with Talia in Afghanistan and they were together when it all went to shit.

The chubby bespectacled man pops open the suitcase, pulls something about the size of a child's hand out, and bends over and fiddles with it.

"Let me have the binocs," I whisper to Dallas. She gives me a look but hands them over.

The device on the end has a metal barb on it about four inches long attached to a small black box with a blinking red light. He carefully places it on the end of the pole and hands it to Talia.

She strides to one of the horse trailers, holds the pole like a weapon, and then with a quick jab, stabs a zombie with it.

With the better view, I can see their arms stick out and the trailer they are close to is rocking more. They are hungry.

This procedure happens one more time at the first trailer and two times at the second.

I feel a chill that has nothing to do with the cold and hand the binoculars back to Dallas. I can feel it, tickling at the edge of my mind. I know what is going on.

Talia left Phantom Ranch and came after us.

Talia found our camp at Wupatki... somehow... and knows we are probably in the 40s.

Talia has taken over this group of survivors. My guess is that Brown is dead. Talia probably pretended to be innocent and wounded, figured out who was in charge, and took him out with extreme prejudice.

And she's going to use the Zs to find us.

Shit. Shit. Shit.

"Those are trackers," I hiss. "The Zs are close enough that they will sense us. They will be able to track the Zs and the Zs will track us."

"Like some kind of bloodhound?" June whispers.

"Exactly like that," I whisper.

We watch as it plays out. Talia and the geek get back in the Jeep and drive off as does the second truck. Two beefy guys get out of the first truck and rig the trailers so they can tug open the doors with ropes. They do it together, opening both doors, the Zs spilling out. They run to the truck, hop into the bed, and the truck speeds away, the squeal of its tires sharp and loud as it cuts through the quiet morning.

The zombies, there are about thirty of them, mill about, but I know it's only a matter of time. Their fungus brains seem to work together somehow. The more zombies there are the more accurate their fresh flesh radars are. It's how the tourist zombie horde followed us down the Grand Canyon. And it's how they've been so effective at finding the living.

The more of them and the hungrier they are the better their "radar" is.

We are so screwed.

CHAPTER SIX

LIFE IS FLEETING.

Even before the Zs came, it was fleeting. A traffic accident could take you out quick or old age could take you out slow with all kinds of things in between. The apocalypse has just brought the fleeting nature of a biological existence into much sharper relief.

Every day surviving the apocalypse, every day with June is a bonus.

This is the other side of the coin of having so much to lose. I have so much to be grateful for.

After Talia and the trucks drive off, I turn around and stare up at the sky. I'm not giving up. I won't ever give up. Not with June and Dallas next to me, but I just need a moment to let it in. Feel it.

Life is fleeting. I am grateful and want more of this life.

I do the math in my head. This is day twenty-six of Woody and June versus the Apocalypse and it's already hard to imagine my life before her.

I just had a few days with good food to eat and June next to me. I've survived more than I thought possible. I have love and friendship. I have lived a life, and despite the condition of the world and some of the shit that has befallen me, it's been a pretty good life.

"They've wandered towards where the trucks were," I say quietly, still facing away. "But they've lost momentum now and they are starting to gather."

"No shit—" Dallas says, but then cuts herself off as she notices I'm not looking at them.

It's a magic trick I'm trying to pull off. A test. I want to know if I understand these beasts as well as I think I do.

The air is calm and cold, the silence deep, but in a comforting way. The stars are slowly fading as the sky lightens from black to the deepest of blues.

"It looks like their movements are random," I continue, still looking away, "like each one is just wandering, but slowly they are coming close, slowly they are forming a tight group, one that seems to be more round than it should be, one that seems more intentional than is possible."

"You're just freaking me out now, Woody," Dallas says.

I just smile.

"How many are there?" I ask.

Dallas is quiet for a moment and all I hear is the gentle breathing of my companions and my heart pounding in my chest. "Twenty-six," Dallas says. "No... twenty-seven."

I see them in my mind, I try to imagine how their fungus brains work. They have a sense for what they need to survive, and when they are together that sense increases. It's like they are each a receiver, and the more receivers in close proximity, the stronger the signal. Kind of like those radio telescopes in the New Mexico desert —working together they are much more powerful.

"Their movements look random," I continue. "They are going this way and that, but they are doing it more or less together now, and from where they started, where they got together, they have moved just a little more towards us than away from us."

"What are you doing?" June whispers. She'd crawled right next to me. "We need to get the hell out of here."

I shake my head. "Not yet. We need those trucks to get farther away. And if we move, the Zs will lock on us. Right now they're not sure yet."

"And how the hell do you know this without looking?" Dallas asks.

I sigh. There's a story, and not a pleasant one. At least not the ending. There was a man in the Phoenix tribe I ended up with that the psychotic, petty, wannabe warlord called "Q." Because he was the gadget guy, the one that could hack tech.

Q took me under his wing and taught me. It's why I could rig the suicide vest I used to recue June and knew all about the drones and how to make phones useful without a cell signal.

Q taught me about the Zs. He was curious about everything. He watched them. He learned.

"I just know," I say, because now is not the time for those kinds of stories. "Dallas, can you please go inside and start gathering our stuff. Move slowly. Don't make any noise. We shouldn't leave until they fully lock on us, but we need to be ready when they do."

I can feel Dallas ready to open her mouth and protest, but she doesn't. My magic trick has worked that well, at least.

After she is gone, June asks, "And what do we do when they lock on us?"

I look at her and smile, her lovely round face dim in the predawn light. "We run, June. We run."

CHAPTER SEVEN

I'M DRIVING the truck across the rough, sandy roads of the 40s. Dallas is in the passenger's seat next to me fumbling with the GPS, looking at the maps and cursing. She's not normally the navigator —she's normally the sharp, colorful commentary from the backseat.

But June is standing in the bed, strapped in like some kind of movie action hero. She's right behind the cab, strapping run through the back windows and around her waist. There are pillows duct-taped to the back window and to the roof. The strap holds her against the truck, and as we jostle along the pillows keep her from getting too badly bruised.

She's standing tall with mirror shades on, holding her rifle. Yeah, the Terminator's Sarah Connor ain't got a thing on my girl.

The zombies took about forty minutes to really lock on. They wandered slowly, unevenly towards us, but then they locked on and as a group started heading directly toward us. The faster ones moving out in front, the sound of their snapping jaws and growls reaching us through the cold, still air.

Dallas had done her job and packed us up. I had rigged the place for June, and we roared out of there.

At the same time, somewhere up the road, I know that Talia's geek noticed the change in the zombies' direction and they started heading this way after us.

The chase is on.

Zombie bloodhounds. Now that's something I would have never thought of. And as much as I hate Talia, I have to admire the innovation, the deep-level understanding of how Zs work and using that knowledge for her psychotic, petty, wannabe warlord purposes.

"I can't work this," Dallas says beside me, stabbing at the phone.

It's a GPS app. One that has map data stored on the phone and doesn't need the internet. As such it's not well designed, not like the mainstream apps we were used to using.

I don't slow down because we don't have the time. Talia won't give up. Talia has taken over Brown's tribe and is using them, a larger, better-equipped group than Phantom Company, to hunt us down.

"There's a blue line ending in a larger blue dot," I say, seeing one of the straw bale houses we explored just coming into view. One of the ones that had the corpses of the living in it.

The land undulates gently, sprinkled with cactus and scraggly juniper trees. A rabbit races across the road in front of us. The sun is nearly up, the land still a bit soft and grey.

"That's us," I continue. "Pinch to zoom in or zoom out. Find the right way through all our wrong turns. Make sure we are following the quickest way out."

"But the damn screen is just green. No roads. No landmarks," she says.

"It doesn't matter," I say. "Just make sure we stay on that line, that we don't miss any turns."

And for the locals, I bet this wasn't complicated. Three or four turns to get into or out of it. But we're being chased and we're out of time and we wound our way through here, making lots of wrong turns, so I can't just follow my tracks back.

And on top of that, I have a terrible sense of direction.

We come to a turn, both directions equally sketchy. These roads were never much in the first place, but now after months of not being used, they are more the promise of a road than a road.

Dallas curses in the seat next to me, but June bangs hard on the left side of the cab.

There. At least June remembers. We speed off.

CHAPTER EIGHT

TALIA ISN'T DUMB. She may be psychotic and petty, and she may be a wannabe warlord, but she is not dumb.

I am. I mean, I can be.

After the Zs lock onto us, we load up into the pickup and head back the way we came. It's quicker this time, we know the way and we aren't making any stops. The sun is just above the horizon when we get close to exiting the 40s, where the disorganized jumble of dirt roads exits onto the two-lane paved road between Wupatki and Sunset Crater. We are all silent and I am driving when we see the assembled group of vehicles waiting for us, and I realize that in this moment I'm the dummy and Talia is not.

Up there on the roof of the Earthship when I was doing my little magic trick proving I understood the Zs, I should have been doing the same thing for Talia. Trying to figure out where her behavior would take her, what she would do.

Of course she had people waiting for us here. She saw our fresh tracks going in and knew that would be how we would likely leave if the Zs spotted us on the other side.

Just like the Zs, the living are driven by our internal needs and desires, a lot of it unconscious. My general view of psychotic, petty, wannabe warlords is they are not very introspective. And this may be pure arrogance, but I think they are more like the Zs in how they operate than we are.

It's this strange, quiet moment, just a second or two. What little hope I had for the day was quickly collapsing under the weight of my realized stupidity. We are just recognizing our foes and they are recognizing us. There is a moment of relative silence as the situation changes from banal to life threatening.

"Shit!" I say, breaking the silence. Dallas offers something much more piquant.

Shots are fired from the assembled trucks in the still cool morning, sounding loud and garish against the peaceful high-desert tableau. Little eruptions of dirt explode around the speeding truck and then I know that Talia is there keeping these shots nonlethal.

She doesn't want us dead, not all of us, at least—not now, at least.

From the pickup truck bed, June returns fires, but just like in the juniper forest near the North Rim of the Grand Canyon, I know she's not aiming to kill. "We are not like them," she said then. Her humanity in the face of the world's madness is one of her most attractive qualities. I mean beyond the pixie beautiful tough-ass warrior woman that she is.

I hit the gas and veer off to the right, off what is left of the road and onto the dried grass, the truck darting between a couple of scraggly junipers that are about eight feet tall.

The windows are down and the dust fills my nose along with the slightly pungent afternote from the trees.

Talia and company are ready for that maneuver, two trucks surging towards us to intercept.

Shots continue to bark out and the adrenaline has filled my veins and I have that clarity that I never experienced before it all went to shit. Things slow down and my vision is sharp and I can see clearly.

Not the future, I can't see that at all, but the here and now. The barely visible line of the painted desert in the distance, colors from light tan to a muddy red, the layers of the desert stacked up to the horizon. The scaly leaves of the juniper plants—unlike the other conifers, they don't have actual needles.

The grim look of determination of the rifleman in the back of one of the trucks trying to intercept us as he swings his rifle around. He's not strapped in, so the jostling as the truck leaves the road knocks him down and he almost falls out.

Dallas next to me whooping and pulling her gun, a whiff of perfume filling my nose. She must have found some in our stashed goods in the truck's bed.

June firing her rifle right above our heads, slow, steady, deliberate.

I make a sharp turn, the road was never my destination once our enemy was spotted, and hope that June is tied in well enough, that all the tubs in back are tied down well enough. I am just turning around and don't want to slow enough for them to go for our tires and disable us.

"Come on, Talia," Dallas yells, leaning out her window and firing in the direction of our pursuit. "I'm ready for you, you skinny-ass sociopathic bitch. You and me, let's do it Old West style and see who is fastest on the draw."

Dallas's antics are like annoying flies. I mean, I appreciate her energy, but that is not what we need now. What we need is a plan.

And, yes, here I am making up a plan in the moment without talking to Dallas or June. But desperate times and all.

I need to look at the maps, but I am driving. I need a moment to think, but we are racing for our lives.

Shots bark out as I roar back onto the dirt road and back into the 40s, three vehicles in pursuit.

And the adrenaline does its job and my mind clears. There has to be personnel on the other end of the 40s too, taking on the Zs they released to hunt us and waiting for us.

"Steer," I shout to Dallas.

She stops shooting and says, "Are you as crazy as the queen bitch of the desert?"

"Nope," I say, but figure that I probably am. "Give me the GPS and steer."

"Don't try to out crazy Talia, Diamondback," she shouts. "We'll all die then."

We can't stop and Dallas can't figure the GPS out. It's the only way. "Do it," I shout, completing our turn around and heading back the way we came.

Dallas leans over, seat belt still buckled, and grabs the wheel with an exquisitely creative burst of curses that speculate as to my origin, my sexual proclivities, and something rather painful I should do with a stick while rotating.

I don't care. I work the phone. I look at the map. I try to tune out the swaying jolting of the truck, the spitting bark of June's rifle and Talia's boys' rifles and only pay attention to the map, to the plan, to Dallas shouting at me to speed up and slow down.

CHAPTER NINE

THE 40S ARE like the reservation in a lot of ways. Sketchy, winding, unmarked dirt roads. Dry desert land. Off-the-grid living. At some point this land, as you head east, turns into the Navajo reservation.

It takes a couple of minutes for me to figure that out, during which we almost flip over twice with Dallas awkwardly steering and me in the driver's seat working the gas and brakes, but we gain some ground on our pursuers.

I take the wheel back and shout my plan to Dallas. "We're going east, taking any damn road we can find, drive over the desert if we have to, and head into the rez. We are going to try to make it to Leupp."

"Where the lights are?" she shouts, really louder than she needs to with the noise, the shooting having slowed down. "Where your Native Americans that have this all figured out and will welcome our white asses with open arms?"

"June is Hispanic," I say. Despite the blue eyes, despite me thinking she might be an Israeli spy early on, much of her lineage is in Mexico.

"So they'll just shoot the two of us," she says, "and welcome cute little June with open arms."

"Tell June the plan," I say, my head jabbing back to the bed. "And we can't stop, but I need her up here to navigate. Figure it out."

I can feel the heat of her stare, it almost feels like my skin should start burning, like she has lasers coming out of her eyes, but she doesn't do more than grumble, unbuckle, and tell me in very colorful terms that I need to hold the truck steady and if I don't what she will do to me.

She crawls into the backseat and shouts at June through the little square window in the back window of the truck. I can't hear it that well so I tune it out and focus on driving.

Hug the corners. Speed up when it's straight. Brake quickly when you need to. Keep an eye on the rearview to make sure our chase team is not gaining too much. Watch the road as it winds over the desolate landscape, rugged houses in the distance. It's hell on the gas mileage, but we've still got some jerry cans filled with gas in the bed.

"You have to stop," Dallas shouts at me from the backseat.

Again, she doesn't have to shout right now, but I just let it slide. It's not the time or the place to quibble about shouting when people are shooting at you.

I shake my head.

"You have to," she shouts. "Find some cover. Slam the brakes on. Give us five seconds for her to get in and for me to get out. That window is too small for even your skinny-ass girlfriend."

I can just see some buildings peeking into view in the distance. One looks like the top of a golf ball, very white.

That will have to do.

I swerve off the main road, such as it is, onto a winding driveway.

"The geodesics dome," I shout. "We'll stop behind it."

Our pursuers are a good hundred yards behind us. Not really enough, but I'm hoping this move gives them some pause, that they wonder if we've set up some kind of defenses here. After all, that would have been the smart thing to do if we had been anticipating Talia as well as I anticipated those bloodhound Zs.

The driveway is cinders, and this could spell death if they get too loose. I go as fast as I dare.

We go up a slight rise around a bend and then I can see that the dome is too far out of our way, but there is another house, looks to be straw bale. Much smaller, but it will have to be enough.

"Hold on!" I shout, taking us off the crappy road and over the desert. Not many junipers. Not much cover. Not much time. But not as many cinders and I should be able to continue going cross-country and get back to the road.

I come to a sliding stop behind the house. Looks like this house burned, the adobe blackened and charred, the windows with just bits of glass left, the roof barely still on. The ladies do their clown-car maneuver, Dallas jumping out and June jumping in. It feels like minutes, no, hours that we are still, but it can't be more than six seconds.

Stopping is where things get dicey for us. If we stop and they are close, they can shoot our tires out without risking an epic crash.

Talia must want June alive. I can't imagine she cares at all about keeping me or Dallas alive.

Sand and cinders fly as I step on the gas and we shoot across the desert.

"I love you, June Medina," I say, flashing her a brief grin.

A smile lights up her serious face. "You better, Woody Beckman."

My smile widens. It's what I told her when she agreed to go with Talia and Phantom Company to save my and Dallas's lives. And it's what she said back.

It's not laughter. Hard to imagine we'll get that today. But it's something. It's a few moments more with her. It's knowing she's by my side. And right now that just has to be enough.

CHAPTER TEN

FROM FLAGSTAFF, US Route 89 wanders north past Sunset Crater and Wupatki. It eventually makes it to Lake Powell and up into Utah. And I-40 heads out east from Flagstaff on its long journey across the country.

Between 89, where we came down from the Grand Canyon, to I-40, where we want to get to so we can head east, there is the undulating cinder-cone-filled land that we are speeding through. As you head east and away from the mountain, you lose elevation and vegetation, the land becoming more desolate and more moonlike.

Somewhere out here they trained with the first moon rover in the sixties. Farther east off I-40 is Meteor Crater, a well-preserved meteor impact site open to tourists... well, when there were tourists.

The whole area has this otherworldly vibe and the views are often spectacular, the land rolling away far into the distance, the varying colors of the dry land and distant mesas breathtaking.

It's the kind of place where you want to walk softly and go slow. Where you want to reflect and breathe deeply of the dry air. Where you want to enjoy the silence and feel the pressures of modern life fall away.

Except the current modern life is fighting zombies and running from psychotic, petty, wannabe warlords, and it's hard to be peaceful when you are being chased and shot at.

Dallas has got herself strapped in the truck's bed, facing backwards. She's shouting and cursing and shooting. And for Dallas, this might just be a pretty good time.

June has got our map spread out over her lap and onto the dashboard with the phone and its GPS app running.

I'm driving, focusing on the moment, trying to keep us going, hoping to avoid losing June again. Well... let's be serious, this time I would be losing my life *and* losing June in the process.

And all we are heading towards is the smallest chance and the thinnest hope that in Leupp we'll find people more reasonable than Talia. That they will be willing to help us. That we can survive this day to face more challenges tomorrow.

"You okay?" June asks gently.

She's managed to guide us farther east, but we've had a couple close calls and lost some ground, a blue Ford F-150 is only thirty yards behind us.

"With you here, I am," I say, trying to smile, but it doesn't work.

"No bullshit, Woody," she says. "Talk to me."

We've come down in elevation, losing the junipers, the land barren, decorated with dried grass and a few small bushes with bits of spring green on both. I'm quite sure we're on the rez now.

When a breeze comes up you can watch it ripple across last year's tan grass like a wave. There's some sagebrush providing a bit more color against the dark volcanic soil.

"Is this ever going to end?" I ask, my grip tightening on the steering wheel even more, my knuckles going white.

Dallas shoots right at the end of my sentence as if to emphasize my point and then she whoops. In the rearview I see steam rising from the F-150—she got the radiator, it won't be chasing us for much longer.

"Is what going to end?" June asks gently, ignoring what is going on behind us at the moment.

We are on a straightaway after curving to the south a bit and I just lay on the gas, flooring it. Behind me I can hear Dallas whoop again.

"Us running for our lives," I say quietly. "Searching. Trying to find a home."

"Of course it's going to end," she says just as quietly. I glance at her and her blue eyes are hard, her lips pressed into a thin line. But then her face relaxes and she smiles. "We found each other, didn't we?"

"And Dallas," I say. "We can't forget Dallas."

Dallas whoops and fires again, her colorful curses floating in the open windows. "Mess with me, bitches, and that's what you'll get."

"No one can ever forget Dallas," June says with a chuckle.

And there it is. June laughed. Well, it was a strained chuckle, but it fully qualifies as my second rule of the day and draws a chuckle out of me.

And my mood lightens. June's right. This will end. We will die today or we will escape and survive. We can only do our best with what we have.

I nod and focus on the dirt road in front of us.

CHAPTER ELEVEN

IT'S glorious having pavement underneath our tires, but our pursuers are desperate.

June navigated us out of the sketchy dirt roads and onto Leupp Road after hours of bouncing through the expansive desert of the Navajo reservation. My bladder is about to burst and my whole body is buzzing from the ride.

To be clear, shooting from one moving vehicle to another is not easy, accuracy being more of a fantasy when those vehicles are bouncing over dirt roads. But paved roads with the shooters in the beds of pickup trucks? Then you can hit something.

As soon as we get on the pavement, June shouts to Dallas, "Get down!"

June worked it out already. She's the soldier. She's the one that spent time in Afghanistan. Forget the fact that if you were putting on a play for kids and needed a fairy, you would cast June in a heartbeat.

"What?" Dallas shouts back.

It's afternoon, we've been at this all day. We're not far from Leupp but we're almost out of gas and with pavement underneath our tires this is now a race. Which vehicle is fastest? How much damage are they willing to do to us?

"Get down before they shoot you," June screams.

The land is volcanic, not flat, but only rolling gently now. There are scattered houses in the distance, simple rectangular houses or the occasional octagonal hogan. There is little more than dried grass for vegetation and the occasional cell tower rising up.

"You too," June says, sliding down in her seat. "Get down. And don't go straight, keep moving from side to side."

Of course she's right. Talia has been playing us, trying to capture us alive. But if we are about to get away, well then, all bets are off.

I scrunch down as much as I can and start swerving across the road randomly. There is blown dirt and dried vegetation on the road, but otherwise it's clear.

We haven't been shot at in a while. I had hoped they had run out of ammo, but that hope is dashed as a series of shots ring out and I hear a loud thunk against the truck and can see Dallas struggling to get loose of the straps that were holding her against the cab so she can get down.

My tired brain wakes up with that.

Where are the rest of Talia's people? Where is Talia? They had time to get people down Leupp Road while we wound our way through the dirt roads of the 40s and the reservation.

I need to use my brain like I did on the Earthship, predicting the Zs' movements without seeing them. I need to do it with Talia.

Dallas is returning fire on the two trucks chasing us from her new position squatting down in the truck bed, using the tubs it is filled with for cover.

Talia is psychotic and petty but she is not dumb. She's been very smart so far.

And then it clicks.

"We need to turn off," I say, my heart clanging in my chest.

"What?" June asks. "Why?"

"Talia's up ahead," I say, nodding down the debris covered road. "She has to be."

June's blue eyes widen and she scans the horizon.

"We're almost out of gas," I say. "Those chasing us must be too. But I bet she's got fully gassed vehicles waiting for us. Think about it, this group know about the people in Leupp. They know how close they can get without starting something. There are no fresh vehicles behind us, so they must be in front of us."

She nods and looks at the maps, except printed maps are not good around here. There are too many barely-there dirt roads going through the rez. I'm pretty sure if you know them, you can get to I-40 from here.

But we don't know them.

And our gas tank is almost empty.

Another shot rings out and my left rearview mirror shatters.

"Turn!" June yells.

There's a dirt road here and one of those simple, rectangular houses in the distance.

I hit the brakes, veer off onto the dirt road, and lean on the gas.

We are so screwed. We have one hope and one hope only. That they run out of gas before we do so we can stop long enough to dump one of the jerry cans into the tank and get moving.

CHAPTER TWELVE

TALIA'S new group has radios. We saw them in use on Mount Elden when the former psychotic, petty, wannabe warlord, Mr. Brown, was in charge (aka Mr. Short and Stocky, aka Asshole). They must have CB radios in all their vehicles. CB is point-to-point communication made to go over long distances and apocalypse-proof.

As we tear south, the gas gauge down past E, my very strange brain thinks of the Smokey and the Bandit movies. Pure cheese and pure car chases, my father loved those movies.

This day is similar in some ways. If they had wanted to kill us, we would be dead by now. They would have shot our tires out causing a hellacious wreck at the speeds we've been traveling and June might not have survived.

This is all about June. Talia wants her back. Down at Phantom Ranch she wanted her back as her partner, now... well, I think it's likely something a lot more twisted, meaning June would be better off dying in a wreck than ending up with Talia.

Which brings me back to the movies. The rules of engagement of that movie was the chase. Smokey never tried to kill the Bandit, just stop and trap him. Which is what Talia is trying to do to us.

Behind us, the two remaining trucks are joined by another truck and a black Jeep. The same black Jeep we saw Talia in when the bloodhound Zs were unleashed to find us.

"Shit," I say, invoking the official word of the apocalypse.

"How much gas?" June asks.

I just shake my head and keep driving. We whip past a single-wide trailer with a few cars in front of it, but it has an abandoned look. It's just bits of spring green poking up among dried grass and rolling dusty roads out here and wispy clouds high in the blue sky.

One of the trucks that has been chasing us falls behind and I see the new truck slow down too. They are refueling.

That thin hope we had is gone, bursting like a soap bubble in a stiff wind that never had a chance.

"I'll go with her again," June says, a slight tremor in her voice. There is not much that scares June, but Talia does. In Albuquerque she faked her death, by zombie no less, just to get away.

And the last time she went with Talia she had to hold a loaded gun to her head to get Talia to let us go. And "letting us go" to Talia meant putting Dallas and me in a situation where we had almost no chance of survival.

"No," I say, my heart beating so hard that I'm afraid that if I look down, I will see my chest vibrating. I can't lose June. I can't.

I'm not a teenager and this is not my first crush. That feeling in me that I can't survive without June feels much more factual. I got lucky being on my own for as long as I did and I don't think I can survive this post-apocalyptic world without her. And I sure as hell know I don't want to.

The other two vehicles, Talia's Jeep and one of the original pick-ups, slow down but they don't stop. They are giving us more room, making it harder for Dallas to shoot another radiator out.

I slow down too, to conserve gas, to give us more time, a few more minutes with June.

"It's the only way, Woody," June says. I steal a glance at her and see so much on her beautiful face. The bruising from her fight with Talia after she gave herself up the first time edging towards purple.

Her lips set in a thin, hard line. Fear in the ocean-blue eyes of hers. And fierce determination.

Well I'm determined too. Determined to keep June or die trying.

And then it hits me.

They've fallen far enough behind that we have just enough time for another clown car maneuver. Not enough time to gas up, but enough time to get me back there with all our gear where I can do something.

Something desperate. Something foolish. Something with long odds of success. But something, nonetheless.

The plan spills out of me in a torrent of words. We don't have much time. June swallows hard, nods, kisses me on the check and crawls in the backseat to tell Dallas the plan.

CHAPTER THIRTEEN

I AM NO ACTION HERO. That would be June with her fearlessness and lithe athleticism and her military training. Or even Dallas with her Montana tomboy upbringing and her wild-as-hell temperament.

Me? I'm a baseball player, have managed to maintain my upper body strength despite the lack of calories, and can sprint just fine, but that's it. My physical grace is limited to the sport I love so much. I was a very good amateur. I loved the feel of the bat hitting the ball, the vibration of it traveling down the bat into my arms. I loved the desperate sprint from base to base and the occasional slide. I loved the cheering of the crowd and the beer shared with friends afterward.

I am no action hero, but I am the gadget guy of the party, so I find myself in the back of the speeding pickup searching through bins and trying to rig something up to save us.

After rescuing June, when we hiked out of the Grand Canyon, we found remnants of a very well-supplied group that had taken up residence there. They had all died, the zombie tourist horde having found them, but we picked through their stuff and put as much as we could in the back of the truck, most of it in big plastic bins.

I have a lot to choose from, but I only need the basics. First some ammunition.

I move some bins to give me some room to work, stacking them up along the back of the truck, providing a bit of a shield. I lay a ratcheting strap over them and tighten it down. This stuff is valuable. We don't want to lose it.

Talia's Jeep and the pickup are still hanging back, banking on us running out of gas, which is their mistake. It does my bruised ego good to see them making one. I've made plenty today.

Behind the bins, shielded from our pursuers, I cut a short piece of strapping and attach it to two carabiners, snapping one to my belt. I make a slightly longer version and hand it through the open window of the truck to June. She smiles and squeezes my hand, but her pupils are a bit too wide—that's what a day of adrenaline will do to you.

I turn away. I can't look at June and do this. I fish out a long piece of tubing, duct tape, and some empty glass bottles from two other bins. I cut a couple of strips of duct tape and tack them to a bin. I pop open one of the jerry cans, put the tube in, and suck on the tube so I can siphon gas into the bottles, getting a mouthful of gas for my troubles.

But what's that compared to the rest of this? The apocalypse has a way of putting things into perspective. It's terrible and I spit it out, but I don't stop. I fill up four empty bottles, keeping them shoved in between a couple of bins so the jostling truck doesn't knock them over.

We still have sticks of dynamite left over from rescuing June from Talia. They are packed very carefully in a large, hard-cased suitcase made of stainless steel. The kind you might see in a spy movie. I flip open the latch and take two sticks out, unwrap them from the bubble wrap they are cocooned in, and set them aside.

Dynamite is a last resort. If it gets used, I need to kill them, kill them all. It would change the dynamic of the battle, the rules of engagement. They are not trying to kill June. We are not trying to kill them. Nothing says "I'm trying to kill you now" like an exploding stick of dynamite.

I set them aside and shake my head, trying to clear it. I can feel June's eyes watching me, but I don't look up at her. I can't.

The truck bounces and that terror I felt wearing the live suicide vest comes back. But we only kept the stable dynamite. It's just my nerves. Except, of course, for the bottles filled with gas ready to spill.

I find rags and a bottle of vodka. I tear the rags into strips, soak them in vodka—it's coconut flavored, which added to the smell of gas is a weird aroma. Then I stuff the alcohol-soaked rags in the bottles and take a big swig of the vodka thinking it will taste better than the gas and maybe shore up my nerves.

I was a beer guy and didn't drink the hard stuff, so I just cough and spit most of it out, but my mouth does taste a little better.

"Shit," I mutter, because I let the seal on the siphon tube go and have to suck on it again. I am more careful, though, and have no more than the caustic fumes of it filling my nose and mouth. I cap the tube with my thumb, clip the other end of the strap I made to one of the truck's tiedowns, and nod to June who is watching from the backseat. "Now," I shout.

She tells Dallas and the little door to the gas tank on the side of the truck pops open.

I pat my jeans pocket and make sure the lighter is there. I check the tubing to make sure the gas is still siphoned up and then I lean over the side of the truck with the tube in my hand, my thumb over that top.

This truck was new when the world ended, so it's a capless gas tank and all I have to do is shove it in. It should be easy.

But this is the action hero part. Leaning out over a moving truck driving at a good speed over a rough road keeping a grip on the tube with my thumb firmly on the top.

The bed wall digs into my stomach. I see the ground flashing below me and dry dust fills my nose. I shove the tube in. I studiously ignore everything else but the task at hand and I push myself back into the bed.

And... nothing. There is air in the tube. The siphon didn't take.

"Here they come!" June shouts.

As expected.

We had found a way to refuel without stopping. As we have established, Talia is not dumb (psychotic and petty, most certainly) and the game has changed. They can't hang back and let us run out of gas because we won't run out of gas.

Peeking through the bins I have stacked in the back, I gauge their distance. There's a little time. I suck the gas up again, dive over the side, stick into the tube in, and dive back.

Nothing.

Damnit.

The shooting starts. I feel a bullet thunking into one of the bins I am leaning against.

"Thirty yards and closing," June yells. "Prepare for plan B."

I nod, crawl over and get one of the Molotov cocktails I created, and fish my lighter out of my pocket. We have a plan B this time. Almost seems like we are getting used to nothing working.

"Twenty-five yards," she yells. "We move in ten seconds."

I start the countdown in my head. I roll my shoulders and loosen up my arm. June moves away from the back window and to the truck's right back door.

I am wishing I had gotten more of that vodka down. That we hadn't stayed at the Earthship and gotten ourselves into this mess. That Talia wasn't such a psychotic piece of work.

When the countdown in my head hits three, I grab one of the bottles and light the alcohol-soaked cloth. It flares to life and I can feel its heat on my hand and my face.

I stay on my knees, so as to not provide too big of a target, and peek through the bins.

I see the Jeep and pickup twenty yards behind. The trucks that have been refueled are a few hundred yards farther back but are gaining. They are getting close. They mean to overtake us.

I rise up on my knees and throw.

At the same time, June does the real action hero stuff and shoves open the truck's door, wedging a sweatshirt in the hinge to keep it open, clipping herself into the handle above the door, and swinging out with her pistol and firing at our pursuers.

Dallas holds the truck as steady as possible.

A dim part of me smiles at this. The three of us working together. Working as a team.

The burning bottle sails towards the black Jeep, its arch graceful. This is the part I am built for. I was never a pitcher, but I have a good arm and I don't have to be perfect here. I stay up long enough for a good follow-through and dive back down.

Shots bark out as June fires on the pickup and the two riflemen in the pickup fire on us. The pickup was her choice of a target. I didn't ask.

Through the bins I see that I overthrew, just a bit, the Molotov cocktail landing on the Jeep's hard roof, fire spreading out beautifully, but Talia doesn't stop.

I light another bottle, rise up and throw, the top of one of the bins I am behind cratering with a bullet hole and flying off.

The second Molotov hits the grill of Talia's Jeep, flames springing up, the Jeep briefly becoming a moving fireball, but the crazy woman doesn't even miss a beat and the Jeep holds steady. I don't know how I can, but I swear I hear Talia cackling over the noise of the truck on the road and the firing of the guns.

June is dangling out of the truck because we figure Talia still doesn't want her dead. The same cannot be said for me. The gunmen in the truck are shooting at me and shooting to kill.

The pursuing pickup darts to the side so I am between June and the truck. Plan C, then. She didn't want to fire on Talia and I didn't want to throw an improvised incendiary device at a pickup with people in the back, but that is what we are down to.

This humanity thing can certainly be an impediment to survival. They are the enemy and I know it. They want to kill me and I know it. And I just want to be left alone.

But they have backed us into a proverbial corner.

I steal a glance back at June. She is glorious, so in her element, where I just want to puke from it all. Her feet are planted in the truck, her right hand holding on to the handle above the door, the other with a gun outstretched and her body leaning out at an angle. The wind is whipping through her short black hair and her ocean-blue eyes are bright with life.

She's dusty and dirty, the wind pressing her black T-shirt tight against her lean body, and I feel something move in me. Yes, she's beautiful and powerful and I want her, but something deeper. She's a beacon to me, like the beam of light from a lighthouse cutting through the night so I can't get lost. She's my reason.

Our eyes meet and a small smile plays on her lips. It's the briefest of moments, but it's enough. I turn back and gauge the distance to the truck. Light my third cocktail up, dart up, and throw.

June is firing. Talia's Jeep is still on fire. The riflemen are firing at me. It all slows for a breath, just a single breath as the bottle turns in the air, the rag burning bright, the sun hot above, the dried grass of the desert whipping by, the smell of gas and vodka and fire filling my head.

A smile spreads across my face and I stay up on my knees longer than I should. The throw is perfect, nothing can ruin this. I feel a lancing pain in my left arm, bright and strong, but I ignore it. I notice both windows of the truck are open. It's an old Chevy, the kind you want in the apocalypse because it's easy to fix and all those little old car problems don't mean anything anymore.

The gunmen dive to the bed. The Molotov hits the windshield square on, fire exploding out and engulfing the truck, some of it getting sucked into the cab. I hear the driver scream and the truck swerves and spins out of control across the desert.

Steam joins the retreating flames of Talia's Jeep. June hit her mark, but the Jeep doesn't slow. Talia will run it until the engine seizes.

I dive down. It feels like something is poking at my shoulder, but I don't have time. There are two more trucks coming, but we have a moment.

I suck on the tube again and dive over the side of the truck, landing hard enough so it feels like a punch to the gut. I keep sucking until I feel the gas hit my tongue and I shove the tube in the tank and push myself back into the bed.

The gas is flowing from the five-gallon jerry can into the tank. Finally.

I grab the duct tape I prepared and dive back over, taping the tube in place and then sag onto the bed floor, my breath coming in ragged gasps.

Through the cracks in the bin, I see Talia's Jeep falling away and the two trucks stopping with her.

I am no action hero, but we did it. It's not over, but we have a moment to breathe.

Why does my arm hurt so much? My hand goes to my left arm and comes away wet with something warm and sticky. Blood.

They shot me.

Dallas steps on the gas and we surge forward.

CHAPTER FOURTEEN

"IT'S JUST A DAMN FLESH WOUND," Dallas says, her full lips pursed dramatically. "Don't be such a baby."

My face is gritted in pain and I can hear the crackle of the hydrogen peroxide that June just poured on the wound, a deep lancing pain jabbing into my arm.

"They shot me," I say, more whine in my voice than I would like.

She snorts, her hands shoved into her jean pockets. "And you firebombed them, Diamondback."

We are in the parking lot of Meteor Crater. The land rises up around the crater so we can't see much but sandy soil and dried grass with bits of spring green poking up. I think this area was originally limestone, the soil being light in color, almost white.

I'm sitting on the tailgate of our truck and June is attending to me. We haven't seen Talia and company since our little action hero sequence, but we know she's out there, we know she's coming.

The quickest way to the White Mountains would be to take I-40 to Holbrook and then head south. But we don't trust it. There's Winslow to get by and Holbrook itself and plenty of little places along the way that could be full of Zs or could be the home to another psychotic, petty, wannabe warlord.

Even before the Zs, Arizona was the kind of state you could get lost in and there are barely-there dirt roads all over out here. So we are going to take them. We are going to try to get lost and hope that Talia doesn't catch up to us again.

There's risk, sure. She could find us. She could get ahead of us. But she could also give up and go back to lording over her minions. And, besides, there's risk at every turn these days. You can't escape it, so you best choose your own path.

Dallas is pacing across the debris covered asphalt like she is channeling our collective unease. Her arms crossed, her brow furrowed, chewing on her lower lip.

June dabs gently at my arm, the wound is just below the shoulder, and while it is a "flesh wound," it hit muscle and it hurts like hell. That hydrogen peroxide, painful as it is, is important. It would be bad if the wound got infected.

We haven't been to the visitor's center yet and we haven't searched the dozen cars here. There must not be free Zs though, or they would have found us by now with the fresh-brains radar.

"Take a swig," June says, handing me the bottle of coconut-flavored vodka.

My mouth still tastes like gasoline. What I need is a little bulb pump so I can stop sucking on gas. Seems like essential equipment these days. We are going to need to be siphoning gas all the way to the White Mountains.

"Why?" I ask, my eyes too wide.

She smiles sweetly. "Because you need stitches and it's going to hurt."

June Medina, legitimate action hero and field medic. Complete with a frank bedside manner and a ready bottle of vodka.

I take a small sip and swish it around and swallow, enjoying the warmth as it goes down, the sharp coconut flavor of it finally driving the taste of gasoline away.

Nobody is saying it this time, but in my heart I know we are not done with Talia. And while the White Mountains are the goal we strive towards, I have no idea if we will get there, and if we do, if it will be what we need.

I smile at June and she raises an eyebrow over one of those ocean-blue eyes of hers. "Why are you smiling?" she asks.

I take another sip and shrug. "Our future is uncertain. There is danger in front of us and danger behind, but... we survived the day. We're together. Seems like that is just about everything these days."

June blinks, her smooth brow furrowing, her gaze falling on the pacing Dallas and then coming back to me. Her lips part and she leans in, but pauses right before our lips meet.

"I love you, Woody Beckman," she whispers.

She doesn't give me time to reply, her lips on mine tasting like coconut vodka.

EPISODE 9
WOODY AND JUNE VERSUS TWO GUNS

More adventure, more zombies, and more Woody and June awaits you in.... *Woody and June versus Two Guns*. Available 10/2022.

To stay abreast of all things Woody and June, head over to WoodyAndJune.com and sign up for my e-mail newsletter and don't miss out on a thing! Plus, you'll get a free ebook that includes "Park's Law of the Apocalypse," a newsletter-exclusive story in the world of Woody and June.

WOODY AND JUNE VERSUS TWO GUNS

One Person's Game is Another's Nightmare

Woody Beckman and June Medina defied the odds and found each other in post-zombie-apocalypse Arizona. No longer go-it-alone survivors, they now face the future together with something to lose. Each other.

When the worst psychotic, petty, wannabe warlord of them all sets a trap for Woody, June, and Dallas and launches them into her twisted "game," it will take everything they've got just to survive the day.

Can Woody and June beat the odds and let their love flourish in a world of zombies and psychotic, petty, wannabe warlords?

A story of adventure and love and taking things (even the apocalypse) in stride.

BEFORE YOU GO

Before you go, my book, *Bits, Bites, and Rarities: The Worlds of Robert J. McCarter* is a fantastic introduction to my series and worlds. It's only available to my newsletter subscribers, and the price is the best part. It's free!

This action-packed book contains 15 stories, is 750+ pages long, and has 4 exclusive stories that are not available anywhere else, including "Park's Law of the Apocalypse," a story in the world of Woody and June you can't read anywhere else.

Get it today at *RobertJMcCarter.com/newsletter*

ABOUT THE AUTHOR

Robert J. McCarter is the author of more than ten novels and over a hundred short stories. He is a regular contributor to *Pulphouse Fiction Magazine* and his short fiction has also appeared in *The Saturday Evening Post, Andromeda Spaceways Inflight Magazine, Everyday Fiction*, and numerous anthologies.

Robert writes in a variety of genres from contemporary fantasy to science fiction and just about everything in between. His diverse background–including a career in software engineering, growing up on a ranch riding horses, and acting–colors the stories he tells.

He lives in the mountains of Arizona with his amazing wife and his ridiculously adorable dogs.

Find out more at:
RobertJMcCarter.com

BOOKS BY ROBERT J. MCCARTER

WOODY AND JUNE VERSUS THE APOCALYPSE

For a great deal, pick up *Woody and June Versus the Apocalypse* a volume at at time!

Woody and June Versus the Apocalypse: Volume 1 (Episodes 1 - 7)

- Woody and June versus the Wannabe Warlord
- Woody and June versus the Fungus-Head Zombies
- Woody and June versus the Grand Canyon
- Woody and June versus the Ex
- Woody and June versus the Third Wheel
- Woody and June versus Phantom Company
- Woody and June versus the Daring Rescue

Woody and June Versus the Apocalypse: Volume 2 (Episodes 8 - 12) *Coming 2/2023*

- Woody and June versus the Chase (coming 9/2022)
- Woody and June versus Two Guns (coming 10/2022)
- Woody and June versus Winslow (coming 11/2022)
- Woody and June versus the Infection (coming 12/2022)
- Woody and June versus the Siege (coming 1/2023)

Find out more at WoodyAndJune.com

NEUTRINOMAN & LIGHTNINGIRL: A LOVE STORY

For a great deal, pick up *Neutrinoman & Lightningirl: A Love Story* a season at at time!

Season 1 (Omnibus edition of Episodes 1 - 3)

- Meteor Attack!
- Toxic Asset
- Protocol X

Season 2 (Omnibus edition of Episodes 4-6)

- Off Book
- Hard Times
- Elemental Factors

Find out the latest at Neutrinoman.com

For a complete list of books, go to RobertJMcCarter.com/books